First American Edition

Library of Congress Catalog Card Number 86-47831
ISBN 0-316-04259-5

First published in Great Britain
by Methuen Children's Books Ltd.

Printed in Hong Kong

Truffles Is Sick

CATHERINE ANHOLT

Joy Street Books

Boston · Little, Brown and Company · Toronto

Truffles woke up in the middle of the night. "I don't feel good," he cried.
"Try to go back to sleep, dear," said Father. "You'll feel better in the morning."

The next morning, Mother brought Truffles his breakfast.
"Oh no, look at those spots!" she cried.

She hurried to call the doctor.

"Cheer up, Truffles," Father said. "You'll feel better in no time."

"He does have a fever," the doctor said.
"It looks as if he'll be in bed for a while."

"Make sure he takes this medicine three times a day."

Tommy stopped by to see if Truffles was ready for school.
"Truffles is sick," Mother told him.
"Could you give this note to his teacher?"

Soon it was time to give Truffles his medicine.
"Don't be such a baby," said Father. "It's not that bad!"

Truffles slept all day.

His friends came to see him after school.
Truffles sat up and waved. "I can't come out today," he called.

Mother made him a cup of tea with honey, gave him his favorite cookies, and read him his favorite book.

"You're right," Truffles said. "Being sick isn't so bad."

By bedtime most of the spots were gone.

"I don't feel too well myself," said Father a while later.
"I think I'd better go to bed."

Mother hurried to the medicine cabinet. "I'll be right back," she called.

"This will make you feel better in no time," she told Father.
"Don't be such a baby. It's not that bad!" said Truffles.